Heather Hammond's
Cool Clarinet

A course for young beginners

Illustrated by Melody-Anne Lee

Cool Clarinet Books 1 and 2 will take you from your very first lesson in Book 1 to around grade 2 level in Book 2. There are many interesting pieces, including some for ensemble playing. There are also exercises to improve technique, listening games and puzzles.

The Teacher's Book has piano accompaniments and the CD provides backing tracks to help you sound great when you practise at home.

Cool Clarinet Repertoire provides an additional range of new and well-known pieces.

Have fun!

kevin mayhew

First published in Great Britain in 2008
by Kevin Mayhew Ltd.
Buxhall, Stowmarket, Suffolk IP14 3BW
Tel: +44 (0) 1449 737978
Fax: +44 (0) 1449 737834
E-mail: info@kevinmayhewltd.com

www.kevinmayhew.com

© Copyright 2008 Kevin Mayhew Ltd.

ISBN 978 1 84417 937 4
ISMN M 57024 852 0
Catalogue No. 3612227

9 8 7 6 5 4 3

Illustration and design: Melody-Anne Lee
Music setter: Donald Thomson
Editor and proof reader: Sarah Stirling
Sound engineer: Christopher Brooke

Printed and bound in Great Britain

Key to symbols

 CD track.

 Complete has clarinet part.

 Backing has no clarinet part.

Exercises that will help you play rhythmically.

Exercises that will help you listen carefully.

Exercises that will help you to get a good sound and help your breath control.

Know the notes

Exercise patterns for getting to know the notes.

Contents

You've chosen to play the clarinet!
Great choice!

You can play lots of different types of music on the clarinet and it's easy to carry around.

In this book you'll learn how to hold the clarinet, get a really good sound, find out how to read music and learn lots of fun pieces.

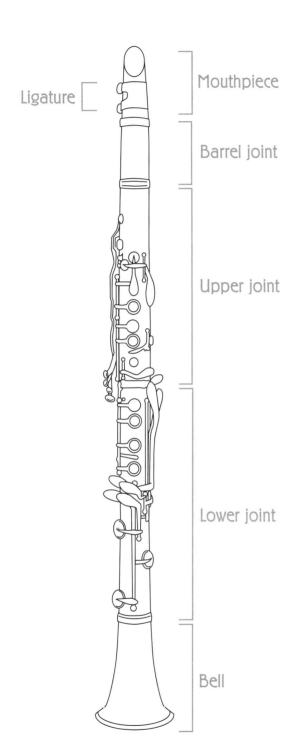

Ligature

Mouthpiece

Barrel joint

Upper joint

Lower joint

Bell

First of all . . .

Your clarinet will be in five pieces. These are:
the mouthpiece (the part that you blow into), the barrel, the upper joint, the lower joint and the bell.

There will also be a mouthpiece cap and a ligature. You will need to get some reeds, cork grease, and a cleaning cloth.

Before you start putting it all together

You must make sure that you have put a little cork grease on all four of the joints where cork is present – this will make it easier for the joints to fit together and will also stop the cork from cracking. You'll need to apply a little cork grease every now and again.

Putting your clarinet together

This must be done very carefully – you don't want to damage your instrument!

Take hold of the upper joint in one hand and the lower joint in the other.

Very important

You need to hold down the rings on the upper joint so that the link piece comes up. It fits over the top of the link piece on the lower joint. Do not press the rings on the lower joint.

Ease the two clarinet pieces together with a gentle twisting motion and make sure that the two link pieces fit together with the lower joint link under the upper joint link.

Then ease the bell onto the lower joint, the barrel onto the upper joint and finally, the mouthpiece onto the barrel.

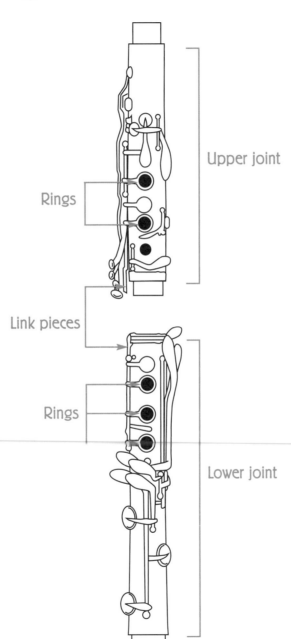

Upper joint

Rings

Link pieces

Rings

Lower joint

The Reed

Select an undamaged reed and put it into your mouth to moisten it. When it is sufficiently moist, place the reed against the mouthpiece, taking care to line up the top of the reed exactly with the tip of the mouthpiece.

The reed is held in place by the ligature – tighten the two screws until the reed is held firmly.

Mouthpiece

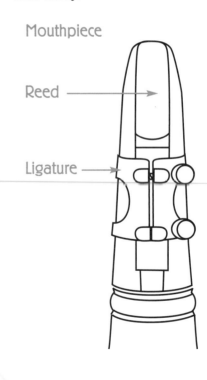

Reed

Ligature

How to hold your clarinet

Thumbs

The right thumb will take most of the weight of your clarinet – it is placed under the thumb rest at the back of the lower joint. Place your left thumb over the thumb hole on the upper joint but don't let it touch the register key.

Back of the clarinet

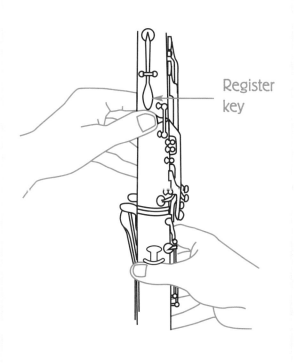

Register key

Fingers

Your fingers should be curled around the clarinet with the pads of your fingers fitting over the holes. Do not let your fingers push against any of the silver keys at the side of your instrument.

Embouchure

(the way you hold your clarinet in your mouth)

Clarinet players have to work really hard to get a good embouchure in order to produce a good sound.

Here are the basic rules. You place your bottom lip over your bottom teeth and rest the reed on the centre of your bottom lip. About one centimetre of the mouthpiece should be in your mouth. Your top teeth now rest on the top of the mouthpiece. Pull your chin down, smile slightly and close the rest of your mouth around the sides of your mouthpiece so that no air will escape out of the sides when you blow your clarinet.

Your teacher will help you modify your embouchure if you need to.

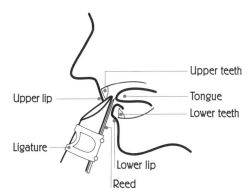

Upper lip — Upper teeth — Tongue — Lower teeth — Ligature — Lower lip — Reed

Posture

Don't hold your clarinet too close to your chest.

Don't hold your clarinet so it's horizontal.

Holding your clarinet halfway between those two positions will be just right.

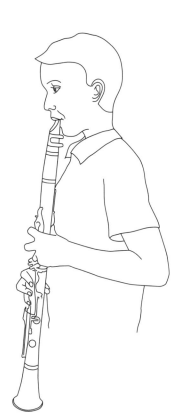

8

Your first sound

Take a deep breath in through the corners of your mouth, then close your mouth around the clarinet and breathe out (try not to let your cheeks puff out).

You may need to experiment for a while before you get a good sound. If you squeak, it could be because your bottom teeth are touching the reed.

When you are making a good sound most of the time, try playing different types of notes.

The sound that you produce will be best if you can play with an open throat.

Try this exercise:
Blow onto the back of your hand – the air will feel cool. Now try it again but this time imagine that you are steaming-up some glass – this time the air will feel warm because your throat was open.

Try to keep your throat open as you play your clarinet (it will take practice).

Long notes

Take a deep breath and blow gently.

Keep the air flow steady and always listen to try and get the best sound. The practising of long notes is really good for clarinet players.

You'll find lots of long-note practice sessions later in this book.

Loud notes

Take a big breath again but this time force the air out quickly. You might not be able to play a very long note because your air supply will run out much quicker!

Short notes

First take a big breath and then put the tip of your tongue onto the reed.

Get ready to breathe out and then move your tongue away from the reed by saying 't'; but then stop the air flow quickly by putting your tongue back on the reed again to stop the sound and make the notes short.

Take a breath when you need to but not between every note.

Soft notes

Begin by taking a big breath but let the air out very slowly and evenly to get a gentle and soft sound.

Keep listening to get the nicest sound you can!

This is a treble clef – you will always find one at the beginning of a line of clarinet music.

Music notes are written on lines and in spaces.
There are always 5 lines and this is called a stave.

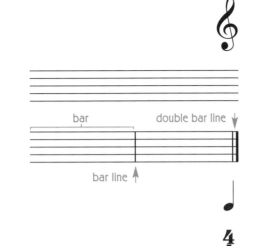

bar   double bar line ↓

bar line ↑

Music is written in bars. They are separated by bar lines.
You will find a double bar line at the end of the music.

This is a one-beat note – a crotchet. You play a sound that lasts for one beat.

$\frac{4}{4}$ You will find 2 numbers after the treble clef. It's called the time signature.
This one tells you that there will be four crotchet beats in each bar.

RHYTHM WORKOUT 1

TRACK
2

It's important to be able to feel a regular, steady beat.
Practise clapping a steady crotchet-beat rhythm along with the track.

SET 1
First note – E

This is what E looks like on the stave

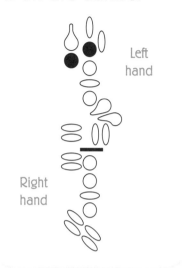

This is how you play
E on the clarinet

Left
hand

Right
hand

Now you can practise keeping a steady
beat again along with the CD track, but this
time play the note E on your clarinet.

Steady Eddie

TRACK
1
COMPLETE

TRACK
2
BACKING

Don't forget to tongue each note at the beginning and just leave a tiny gap
between each note – make sure the silence between the notes is not too long.

 ## Just E-soft and slow

Soft and slow

12

Just E-loud and fast

Loud and fast

If you are having problems getting a good sound get your teacher to check your instrument and reed are OK.

This is a crotchet rest.
You have to be silent for one beat.

Practise clapping each of the following rhythms four times. Then clap the whole thing through twice with the CD accompaniment.

This sign tells you to be silent for a certain number of bars in the music. This one means don't play for four whole bars. Often another instrument will be playing whilst you are being silent.

In the next piece don't play anything for the first four bars – listen to the piano introduction and then start playing at bar 5 – you'll need to count really carefully!

Bluesy E

TRACK 7 COMPLETE   TRACK 8 BACKING

13

What's become of E?

Thoughtfully

14

 This is a two-beat note – a minim.

This is a minim rest – you have to be silent for 2 beats (It sits on the middle line of the stave).

 RHYTHM WORKOUT ③ TRACK 2

Practise clapping the following rhythms four times. Then clap the whole thing through twice with the CD accompaniment.

1   **2**

3   **4**

To make really good progress try to practise your clarinet every day.

Sunset beach

Reggae style

When you first start learning to play you may get tired. Just put your clarinet down for a while and have a short rest.

Music quiz

Let's see how much you have learnt about music so far.

Write your answers in the boxes below

1. How many beats is this note worth?

2. What is this sign called?

3. How many lines are there on a stave?

4. How many beats will there be in each bar? $\frac{4}{4}$

5. What is a two-beat note called?
(clue: you can read this word backwards too!)

6. For how many beats should you rest when you see this sign?

7. What are these called?

8. For how many beats should you rest when you see this sign?

How many did you get right?
If you got some wrong see if you can find the
answers in Set 1 before going on to Set 2.

SET 2
Next note – D

This is what D looks like on the stave

𝗼 This is a four beat note – a semibreve.

Know the notes

Practise each of these patterns four times.

This is how you play D on the clarinet

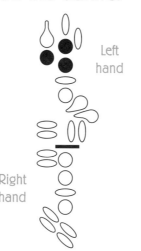

Left hand

Right hand

Lightly squeeze the necessary keys to get the note that you need.

The fingers not being used should be positioned close to the holes or gently touching the rings but not actually pressing them down. See page 7 for finger positions.

When you take off your middle finger (going to E after playing D) just move it the smallest amount possible and try to ensure that your fingertip keeps contact with the ring.

If you move your fingers as little as possible you'll be able to play fast pieces eventually.

Winter morning

TRACK **13** COMPLETE TRACK **14** BACKING

Gently

Sunrise island

Allegro

18

Listening game 1 TRACK 17

Using the notes E and D listen to the CD and try to copy the tunes like an echo.

When you learn about music you also have to learn to speak some Italian.
Many of the words that tell you how the music should be played will be written in Italian.

piano is the Italian word for **soft.** It is written in the music as p.

forte is the Italian word for **loud.** It will say f on your music.

Just practise for short amounts of time when you first start learning to play clarinet.

Cloudy skies

With sadness

Wordsearch fun!

See if you can find the following musical words in the wordsearch.

CLEF	CLARINET	NOTES	PIANO
REST	MINIM	MUSIC	BAR
FORTE	STAVE	BEAT	TREBLE

M	I	N	I	M	U	B	E
B	E	A	T	U	O	A	T
N	O	T	E	S	S	F	R
O	E	R	P	I	A	N	O
A	F	E	R	C	L	E	F
W	A	B	A	R	E	D	A
R	S	L	P	T	S	E	R
S	M	E	V	A	T	S	N
T	E	N	I	R	A	L	C

This is a whole bar's rest. It hangs from the 4th line of the stave.

Don't worry too much if you don't make a perfect sound every time you play. It takes lots of practice to get a really good tone.

Get ready

TRACK **20** COMPLETE

TRACK **21** BACKING

Cheerful

Pupil

* Optional 2nd part

Now try these pieces from Cool Clarinet Repertoire Book 1
Far away p.4
Keep on smiling p.5

Optional part for your teacher

SET 3
And now for – C

When you run out of lines on the stave because you want to play notes even lower or higher, you can just add extra lines to put the notes on. These are called leger lines.

 This is a half-beat note – a quaver.

This is what C looks like on the stave

 Two of them together are played in the time of one beat.

This is how you play
C on the clarinet

Left hand

Right hand

 **Know the notes**

Practise each of these patterns four times.

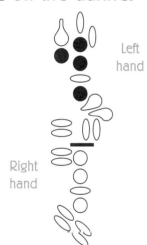

1

2

3

Cowboy's swing

TRACK 22 COMPLETE   TRACK 23 BACKING

Laid back

Practise clapping the rhythms four times each. Then clap the whole thing through twice with the CD accompaniment.
If you want to go at a steady speed use CD track 2 but for a faster challenge use track 6 instead.

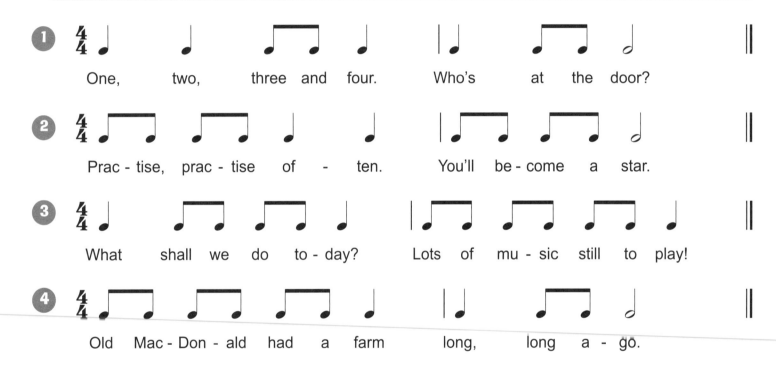

1 One, two, three and four. Who's at the door?

2 Prac - tise, prac - tise of - ten. You'll be - come a star.

3 What shall we do to - day? Lots of mu - sic still to play!

4 Old Mac - Don - ald had a farm long, long a - go.

22

 Listening game 2

TRACK 24

Using the notes E, D and C listen to the CD
and try to copy the tunes like an echo.

Breathe in through your mouth – not your nose!

Funky Mikki

23

Capital city problem!

Can you match the capitals with their countries using their correct rhythms?

Capital cities: Amsterdam / Paris / London / Rome / Copenhagen / Washington D.C.

Write your answers in the boxes below.

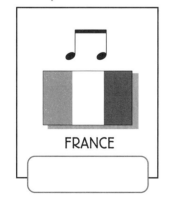

FRANCE

DENMARK

ITALY

UNITED KINGDOM

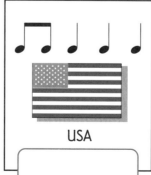

USA

NETHERLANDS

A piece of music with 3 beats in every bar is sometimes called a waltz.
Allegro means quick and lively.

William's waltz

* Optional part for your teacher

24

Now try these pieces from
Cool Clarinet Repertoire Book 1

Mary had a little lamb p.5
Starlight nocturne p.6
In the light of the moon p.6

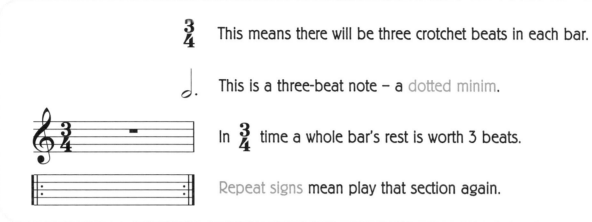

3/4 This means there will be three crotchet beats in each bar.

♩. This is a three-beat note – a dotted minim.

In **3/4** time a whole bar's rest is worth 3 beats.

Repeat signs mean play that section again.

Heading south

TRACK **29** COMPLETE TRACK **30** BACKING

Allegro

Take special care with your reeds. They are very delicate and easily damaged.

SET 4
Here's – F

This is what F looks like on the stave

This is how you play
F on the clarinet

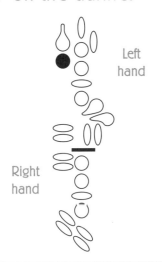

Left hand

Right hand

Practise each of these patterns four times

1

2

3

4

((•))) Listening game 3 TRACK **31**

Using the notes C, D, E and F listen to the CD and try to copy the tunes.
They all start on F.

Don't forget to check whether you should be playing loudly *f* or softly *p*.

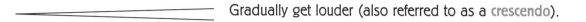 Gradually get louder (also referred to as a crescendo).

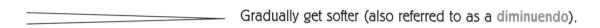 Gradually get softer (also referred to as a diminuendo).

If there are only end repeat signs written you go right back to the beginning of the piece and play again.

Try these exercises to help you gradually change your loudness.

Practise starting softly then gradually increase the air pressure and get louder throughout each bar. Take a breath each time you begin a new bar.

Practise starting loudly then gradually getting softer in each bar. You'll have to judge exactly how much air pressure to use to get a loud note that sounds good.

Next try making one long note gradually get louder. Remember to start each note by saying 't' gently and then gradually increase the air pressure throughout each four-beat note.

Start each note loudly then gradually get softer here.

Finally play this short tune to practise gradually getting louder and softer as you play lots of different notes.

Always wipe off the moisture from your clarinet after you have finished playing.

Andante means play at a medium walking speed.

Auntie's andante

Andante

Pupil

* Optional 2nd part

* Optional part for you teacher

D.S. al Fine means return to the 𝄋 sign and then finish where it says 'Fine' (pronounced 'fee-nay'). It means 'the end' in Italian.

Medieval march

30

Strange horizon

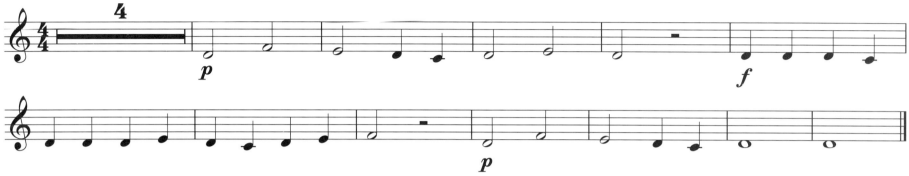

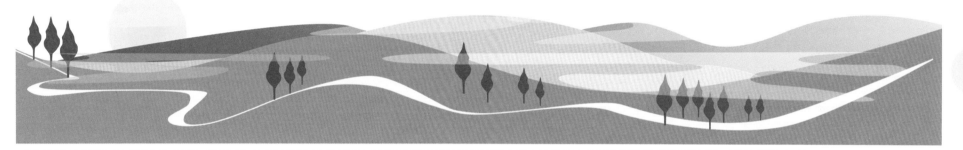

Long 1
note practice

Play these long notes along with the CD. Try to make a really good sound. Breathe after each note if you need to.
Start playing after the 8-beat drum introduction.

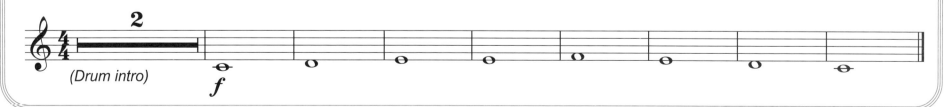

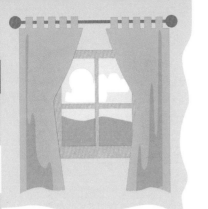

mezzo forte (*mf*) means play quite loudly – not as loudly as *f* though.

mezzo piano (*mp*) means play quite softly – not as softly as *p* though.

Monday morning waltz

TRACK **38** COMPLETE   TRACK **39** BACKING

32

Check that you are still tonguing. Remember to say 't' as you play each note.

Now try these pieces from
Cool Clarinet Repertoire Book 1

Brave and bold p.7

Feelin' sad p.8

Crossword fun

First see how many answers you know without looking back in the book. If you do get stuck, all of the answers can be found earlier in this book.

1. The name of a two-beat note.
2. This means 'quite soft' in Italian.
3. This appears at the beginning of the music and tells you how many beats there will be in every bar.
4. A piece of music with 3 beats in every bar is sometimes called this.
5. The time name of this note.
6. The name of a note that is worth only half a beat.
7. This Italian word means 'medium walking speed'.
8. This Italian word tells you to play loudly.
9. What must you do for a whole bar when you see this sign?
10. How many beats is a minim worth?
11. Music is split into these with bar lines.
12. How many beats is this note worth?

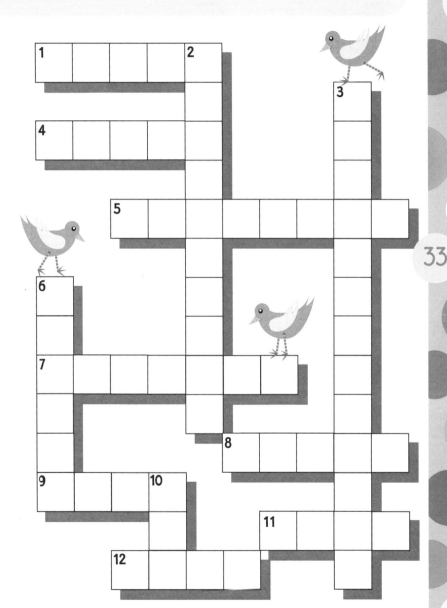

33

SET 5
This is – G

This is what G looks like on the stave

This is how you play G on the clarinet

Clarinet players often refer to this G as *open G*

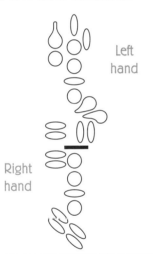

Left hand

Right hand

34

1

2

3

4

RHYTHM WORKOUT 5

Practise clapping each of these rhythms four times. (Watch out for the rests!)
Then clap the whole thing through twice with the CD accompaniment. For a steady speed use track 2, for a faster speed try track 6.

A curved line above or below two notes with the same letter name is called a *tie*. You add the two note values together and just play one note.

So  is worth 3 beats and is held for 5 beats.

Lazy weekend waltz

TRACK 40 COMPLETE   TRACK 41 BACKING

Flowing lazily along

mp

f

p

Now try these pieces from
Cool Clarinet Repertoire Book 1

Merrily we jazz along p.8
Girls and boys p.9

Make sure that you are listening to what you play – it's easy to forget when you are concentrating really hard while reading the music.

60 seconds ballad

Pop ballad

Long note practice 2

(2 bars drum, 2 bars piano intro)

36

Breathe when you need to – if necessary make a long note slightly shorter in order to grab a breath.

Rockin' at rock pool bay

Now try these pieces from
Cool Clarinet Repertoire Book 1

When the saints go marching in p.10
Ode to joy p.11

Quiz time

At Rock Pool Bay the ice-cream seller has forgotten which flavour each of the ice creams are. Can you use the rhythms to help him work out which is which?

Flavour	Ice-cream number
Tutti-frutti	
Neapolitan	
Choc-chip cookie	
Bubblegum	
Marshmallow	
Blueberry pie	
Toffee	
Mint	
Apple pie and custard	

SET 6
And next is – A

This is what A looks like on the stave

This is how you play
A on the clarinet

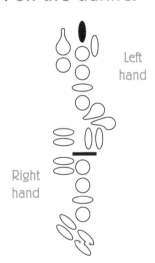

Left hand

Right hand

Notice A is played with
the side of the finger

1

2

3

39

4

Quavers can sometimes
be grouped in 4's

When moving to A from a note lower than G, rotate your forefinger gently onto the A key in a smooth movement.
If you make a jerky movement you may hear the G note first before you get the A.

 Listening game **4**

TRACK **47**

Using the notes E, F, G and A listen to the CD and try to copy them.
The first one starts on F.

Now try these pieces from
Cool Clarinet Repertoire Book 1

Lavender's blue p.12
This old man p.13

Frisbies

TRACK **48** COMPLETE

TRACK **49** BACKING

40

Gliding along

Remember this is a tied
note worth 6 beats

Practise clapping each of these rhythms four times. Then clap the whole thing through with the CD accompaniment. Watch out for the rests!

Kit bag blues TRACK 51 COMPLETE TRACK 52 BACKING

Fast

41

Clowns' parade

* Optional part for your teacher

Now try these pieces from
Cool Clarinet Repertoire Book 1

Lucky boots bossa p.14
Frère Jacques trio p.16

Happy or sad? Correct or wrong?

The clowns have been learning about music but they've got some of their information wrong. Can you help them to sort out their facts?

If the clown's information is correct draw a happy mouth and colour his hat yellow. If the clown's information is wrong draw a sad mouth and colour his hat red.

SET 7
Now for – F sharp

This is what F sharp (F#) looks like on the stave

 This is a sharp sign – it makes the note slightly higher than it usually is.

 This means there are two crotchet beats in every bar.

 This is a key signature. It is telling us that all of the F's in the pieces will be F sharps! (not ordinary F's).

This is how you play F sharp on the clarinet

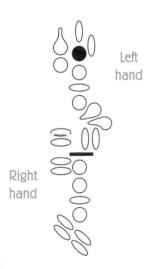

Left hand

Right hand

Try this exercise so that you can hear how F sharp sounds compared with an ordinary F.

Know the notes   Practise each of these patterns four times.

↓ Don't forget the F sharp!

Before you start to play always check the key signature to see if you should be playing any of the notes as sharps.

Diminuendo is the Italian word for gradually get softer. It is sometimes abbreviated to dim.

Crescendo means gradually get louder. It will sometimes just say cresc. in the music.

D.S. al Coda means go back to the 𝄋 sign. You then play until you reach the To Coda ⊕ instruction. Then go to the coda (the end section).

 A dot either below or above a note tells you to play it as a really short note. It's called staccato.

♮ This is a natural sign. It cancels out sharps and tells you to play the normal note instead.

In the next tune there are lots of short notes for you to practise your staccato playing, and a mixture of F sharps and F naturals.

Grandma's ragtime rave-up

Now try these pieces from Cool Clarinet Repertoire Book 1   Boogie woogie jingle bells p.18   The team's lament p.19

Sleepy eyes

46

Mrs Muddle's mix-up

Oh dear! Mrs Muddle seems to have got all of her musical words mixed up.
Can you help her to unscramble them?

MRS MUDDLE'S WORD	CLUE	REAL WORD
D O N U D I N I E M	this means gradually getting softer	
P A R S H	the sign that makes the note slightly higher	
A D O C	the ending	
G E L A R O L	the Italian word for quick and lively playing	
V A Q U E R	a note worth half a beat	
D A N E A N T	play at medium walking speed	
B E M I V E S T E R	a note worth 4 beats	
A L U T A R N	cancels out sharps and flats	
O C C E R N E D S	gradually getting louder	
C A T O C A S T	this means play a short note	
T I L N E S	use your ears to do this whenever you play music	

SET 8
Here is – B

This is what B looks like on the stave

This is how you play B on the clarinet

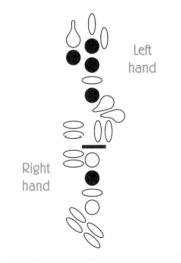

 Practise each of these patterns four times.

48

Always use an undamaged reed and make sure that it is positioned correctly.

When sharps or naturals appear beside the notes rather than in the key signature they are callled accidentals. When accidentals appear their effect lasts for the whole bar unless another accidental sign is introduced to change the note again. In the next piece the F# in bar 8 is a cautionary sign to remind you to stop playing F naturals and go back to playing F sharps again after the bar line.

Moderato means play at a moderate speed.

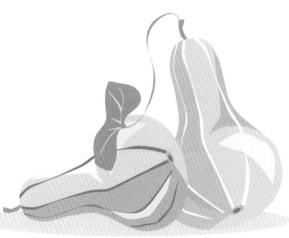

Butternut bossa

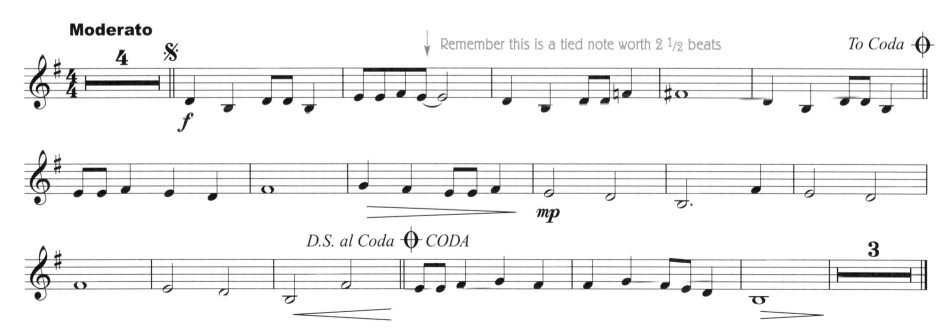

Moderato

Remember this is a tied note worth 2 ¹/₂ beats

To Coda

Long note practice 3

Play these long notes along with the CD. Try to get the best sound that you can.

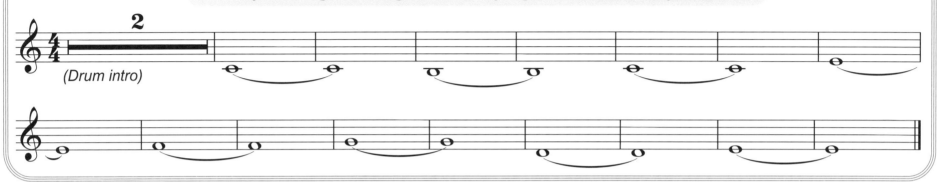

(Drum intro)

Keep a steady beat – Tapping your foot along with the music may help.

RHYTHM WORKOUT 7

TRACK 2 TRACK 6

Practise clapping each of these rhythms four times. Then clap the whole thing through twice using your choice of accompaniment.

1. Won - der - ful,   that's   won - der - ful.

2. Don't   let the mu - sic   stop.

3. Won - der - ful,   tru - ly won - der - ful.   That's

4. What   we   like.   Like it   a lot!

Now try these pieces from   While shepherd's watched their flocks p.19   Annie's song p.22
Cool Clarinet Repertoire Book 1   Cop chase p.20

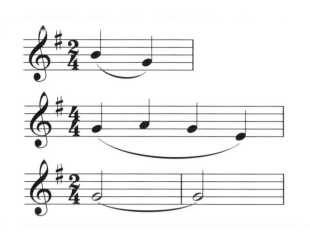

This is a slur. It tells you to play smoothly. You tongue the first note then move smoothly to the next note without tonguing it. It is sometimes called playing legato.

Slurs can also be placed above or below lots of notes.
Just tongue the first one.

Don't forget that the same sign is used for tied notes too but both notes have to be the same letter name for it to be a tie.

Wonderful

Relaxed moderato

TRACK **64**

Using the notes D and E, F♯ and G listen to the phrases on the CD and try to copy them. The first one starts on G.

> This is an accent. You play the note with extra force.

Aliens' clog dance

TRACK **65** COMPLETE   TRACK **66** BACKING

52

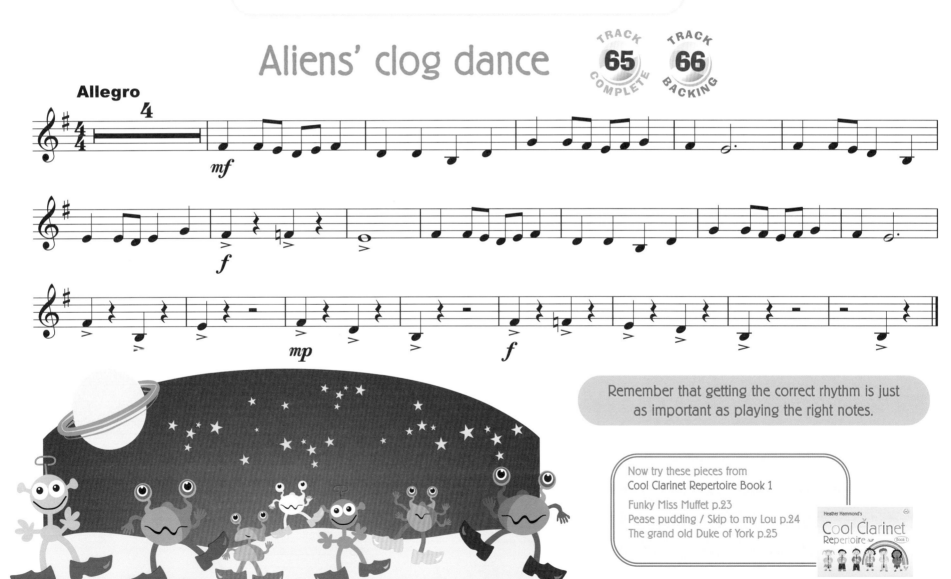

Remember that getting the correct rhythm is just as important as playing the right notes.

Now try these pieces from
Cool Clarinet Repertoire Book 1

Funky Miss Muffet p.23
Pease pudding / Skip to my Lou p.24
The grand old Duke of York p.25

Heather Hammond's
Cool Clarinet
Repertoire

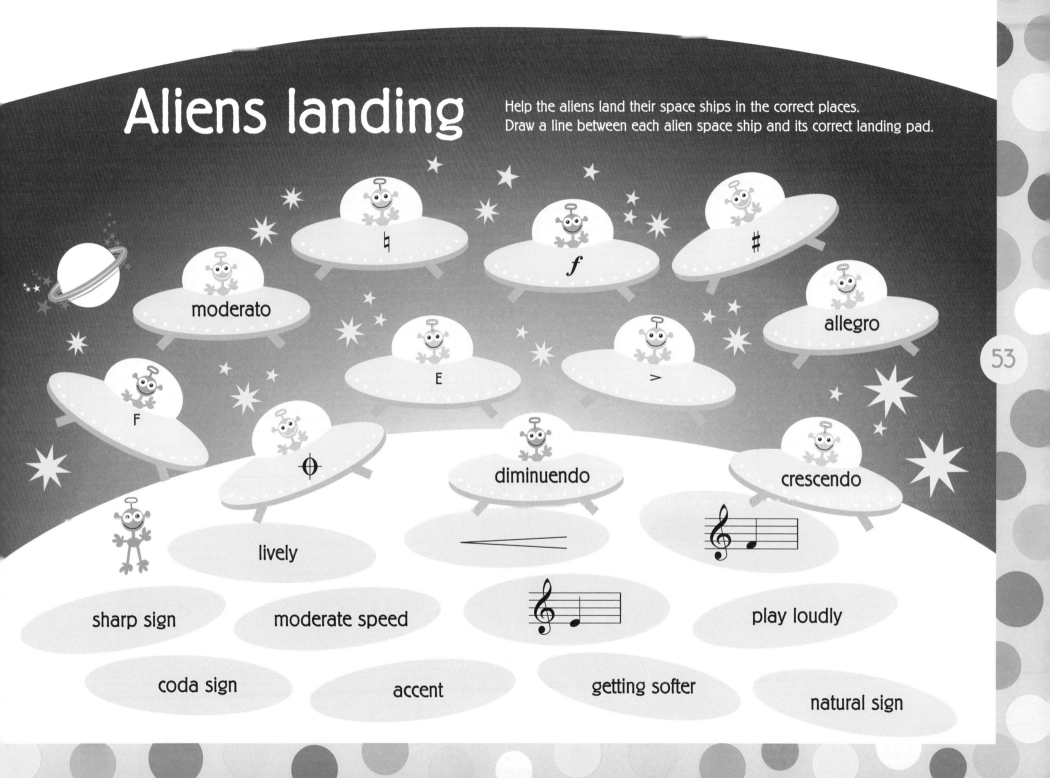

SET 9
Introducing – B flat

This is what B flat (B♭) looks like on the stave

 This is a flat sign – it makes the note slightly lower than it usually is.

 This key signature tells us that all of the B's in the piece will be B flats (not ordinary B's).

This is how you play **B flat** on the clarinet

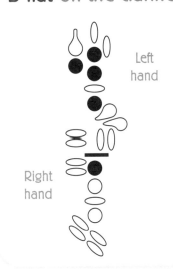

Left hand

Right hand

 **Know the notes**

Practise each of these patterns four times. Remember to play slowly at first.

1

2

3

4

54

TRACK 2 **TRACK 6**

Practise clapping each of these rhythms four times with a friend or your teacher. Count carefully. Do a second time but change parts. Then clap the whole thing through using your choice of accompaniment.

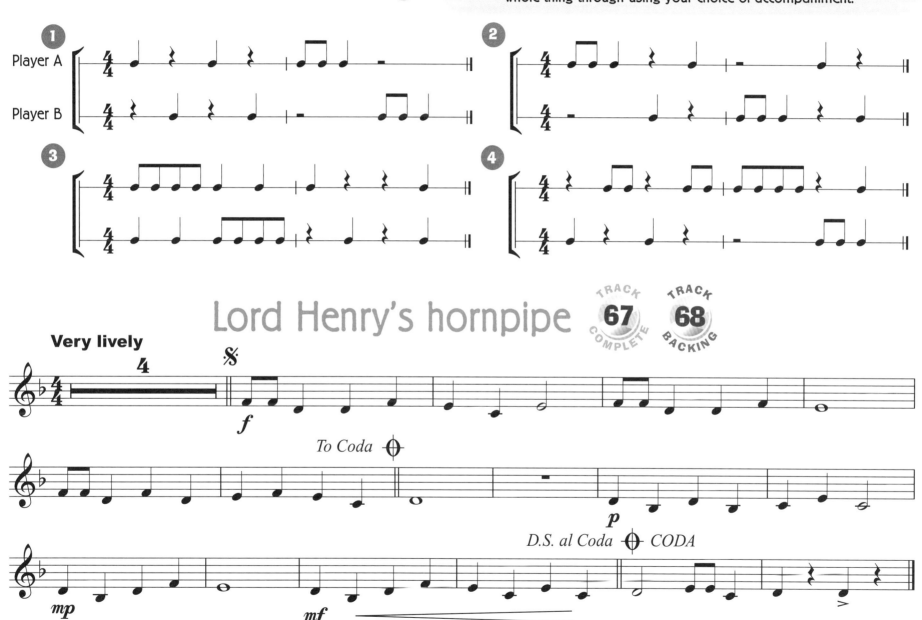

Lord Henry's hornpipe

TRACK 67 COMPLETE **TRACK 68 BACKING**

Very lively

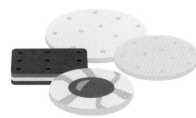

Grandma's biscuit tin

Jazzy allegro

56

To Coda

mf

f

mf

f

mp

D.S. al Coda CODA

cresc.

mp

Now try these pieces from
Cool Clarinet Repertoire Book 1

Bluebirds p.26
Synco-rock 2 p.27

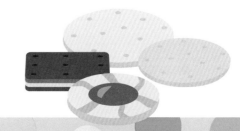

SET 10
Time to learn – C sharp

This is what C sharp (C#) looks like on the stave

This is how you play
C sharp on the clarinet

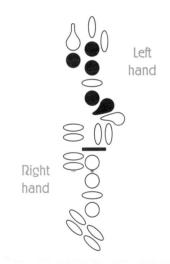

 **Know the notes**

Practise each of these patterns four times.
Remember to play slowly at first.

1

2

3

4

1st time and **2nd time bars** – when you play the music the first time go to the 1st time bars, you then have to go back to the repeat sign.

When you are playing through for the 2nd time miss out the 1st time bars and go directly to the 2nd time bars.

⌒ or ⌣   This is a **pause** sign. It tells you to hold the note for a little while longer than it is actually worth.

Boogie pants

With a driving Boogie beat

 **6**

TRACK 73 Using the notes C♯, D, E, F and G listen to the phrases on the CD and try to copy them. The first one starts on D.

58

This key signature is telling us that all of the F's will be F sharps and all of the C's will be C sharps in the piece.

Long
note practice 4

TRACK 74

Play along with the CD. Don't forget to concentrate on getting the best sound that you can.

remember this note will be a C sharp because of the key signature

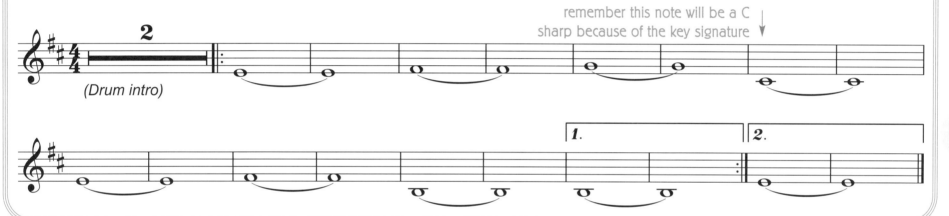

(Drum intro)

If you find a new piece difficult when you first start practising it – just go very slowly for a while. As you get to know the piece more you'll gradually find that you can play it at the correct speed.

Now try these pieces from
Cool Clarinet Repertoire Book 1

Sneaky shot p.28   Just can't wait p.31
Wishing on a star p.29   Mrs Muddle p.32
Mango tango man p.30

Heather Hammond's
Cool Clarinet
Repertoire ~ Book 1

rall. means becoming gradually slower.
It is short for the Italian word rallentando.

a tempo tells you to return to the original speed again.

Ballad for Mr Blue

TRACK **75** COMPLETE TRACK **76** BACKING

Gently flowing

Sounds familiar?

Can you add the missing items to complete this well-known tune?

1. Put in a time signature that means 4 crotchet beats in every bar.
2. Add an F worth 1 beat.
3. Add a C crotchet.
4. Add a bar line.
5. Add an F worth 3 beats here.
6. Add a C worth 2 beats.
7. Add a rest worth 1 beat.
8. Add an F worth 1 beat.
9. Add 4 crotchet F's in this bar.
10. Add an F crotchet here.
11. Add a C minim here.
12. Add a G crotchet.
13. Add an F worth 4 beats.
14. Now play the tune.
15. Add the title above the tune.

Song title:

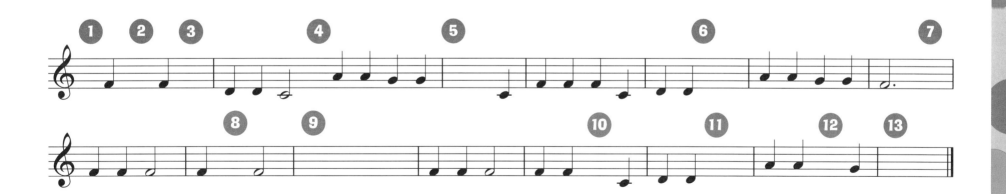

Engineer's rag

62

Never dance with an elephant!

This is to certify that

_____

has successfully completed
Cool Clarinet Book 1
and is now promoted to **Cool Clarinet Book 2**

_____

Teacher

_____

Date